Pelham Pictorial Sports Instruction Series

Brian Jacks

JUDO

Pelham  Books

Also in the Pelham Pictorial Sports Instruction Series

Chester Barnes: Table Tennis
Henry Cooper: Boxing
John Dawes: Rugby Union
Bob Wilson: Soccer
Barry Richards: Cricket
Ken Adwick: Golf
Richard Hawkey: Squash Rackets
Rachael Heyhoe-Flint: Women's Hockey
Jack Karnehm: Understanding Billiards and Snooker
Paul and Sue Whetnall: Badminton

In preparation

David Haller: Swimming

First published in Great Britain by
PELHAM BOOKS LTD
52 Bedford Square,
London WC1B 3EF
1976

ISBN 0 7207 0922 9

Filmset and printed in Great Britain by
BAS Printers Limited, Wallop, Hampshire

Contents

Foreword

by Charles Palmer, O.B.E.,
President of the International Judo Federation,
Chairman of the British Judo Association,
Secretary General of the General Assembly of
International (Sports) Federations.

The judo of Brian Jacks is very active, stylish and above all effective. Since he first became an international, winning a European title in 1964, my task of organising judo all over the world has been given added pleasure through seeing Brian fighting for Britain.

Brian's book illustrates vividly some of the techniques which have brought him so many well-deserved successes and I'm sure it will be read avidly by experienced judomen and beginners alike.

Brian's years at the top have coincided with the growth in the popularity of judo, now an established Olympic event and widely practised by men, women and children all over Britain. I hope this book will encourage still more to participate in this deeply rewarding sport.

C.P.

Introduction

Judo is an exciting, deeply satisfying sport which provides a superb method of keeping fit for all ages. In my classes I see sixty-year-olds and six-year-olds performing with equal zest and enjoyment. I have devoted the past twenty years of my life to judo and it has given me much in return — not only trophies and titles but friends, travel and many good times.

In this book I describe the techniques which have brought me success. After setting out the basic moves I illustrate combinations which stem from them and which form the basis of my judo. The emphasis is on throwing but I also show how to hold down, strangle and arm-lock an opponent.

I must emphasise the importance of receiving sound instruction at a reputable club. The governing body of the sport in Britain is the British Judo Association. If you write to them at 70 Brompton Road, London, S.W.3, they will give details of the clubs near you. When I was a teenager my father encouraged me to train at all the main London clubs but my preference was for the Budokwai in South Kensington. After learning so much from the other instructors there over the years I am now honorary Chief Instructor.

My first international competition at the age of 17 in East Berlin. Receiving the gold medal and Junior European middleweight cup

I would like to describe briefly my judo career and explain how the techniques I have written about have evolved. I first started judo at the age of ten along with my father, who was worried about his increasing weight: he earned his living as a taxi driver. At this time I was interested in many other sports and only began to specialise in judo when my father won a medal in competition — I wanted to get in on the act!

Judo

One of the proudest moments in my judo career: just prior to receiving the Olympic bronze medal in 1972 from Charles Palmer O.B.E., President of the International Judo Federation

I began to train seriously and my father — he is now a 2nd Dan Black Belt — realised I had potential and arranged for me to stay in Japan. I went to Tokyo when I was fifteen and stayed for two years, training at universities and high schools and trying to copy the judo of the Japanese masters.

The hard work paid dividends, as it always does, and on my return I won the European Junior Middleweight title in 1964 and 1965 and represented Britain in the 1964 Olympics, when I was seventeen. But the proudest moment was to come eight years later, when I won a bronze medal at the Munich Olympics.

At the beginning of my contest career (I have now taken part in some three hundred international matches) the strongest part of my judo was groundwork (*ne-waza*). Later I did well with the body drop throw (*tai-otoshi*), and when my opponents began to get used to this I developed my inner thigh throw (*uchi-mata*) and shoulder throw (*seoi-nage*). During normal practice sessions my main objective is to improve my judo. I leave contest judo for actual contests and work to improve my speed and technique and not necessarily to beat my opponents. It is also important to practise at a variety of clubs and meet opponents of different grades with varying styles and physiques. I find that practising with the same people not only becomes boring but also takes the edge off my particular style, since my opponents' reactions become especially conditioned. Always think carefully and analytically about your judo. Ask others to watch you and make suggestions on how you can improve your style.

I start to think about and prepare for a big contest up to three months beforehand. For the first two months I practise five nights a week, for about two hours each night, and try to work as hard as possible. I also run two or three miles each morning and do a lot of stretching and suppling exercises. Every other day I include a light weight-training session. I always enjoy swimming, and, at this stage, I do quite a lot of continuous swimming, often up to a quarter of a mile.

In the month before the contest I take part in other sports which are good for judo fitness — such as badminton, gymnastics and trampolining. I feel it is very important for me to relax sometimes during this pre-contest period and to this end I play golf. I still practise judo five nights a week, but only for an hour, and I make it lighter and looser than before. I cut down on the frequency of my running, but I still run quite hard and visualize my opponents and contemplate how I am going to make them pay for making me work so hard prior to the competition.

In the final week before the contest I may run a little, but not hard enough to affect my store of nervous energy. In the actual event I concentrate entirely on throwing my opponent, and I don't worry about what he might do to me.

As I have said, judo can be enjoyed at all levels but those who aspire to be top-contest men must be prepared to train hard and often.

To all my readers, beginners and Black Belts alike, I hope this book will make your judo more effective and enjoyable.

About Judo

It is generally accepted that judo originates from the various forms of jujitsu used by the *samurai* (warriors) in Japan's violent, feudal past. These often brutal self-defence systems were distilled into the sport of judo by Dr Jigoro Kano who opened the legendary Kodokan club in 1882. The first club in Europe was the Budokwai which was opened in London by Gunji Koizumi in 1918. The first European championships were in 1951 and the first world championships in 1956.

The Japanese dominated the sport until 1961 when, in Paris, the giant Dutchman Anton Geesink defeated the formidable Japanese Kaminaga, Koga and Sone to win the world title. In those days there was only one weight category and the fact that Geesink was 6 ft 6 in. tall and weighed 19 stone no doubt helped. But he was also very fast and skilful both in standing and groundwork. At the 1964 Olympic Games in Tokyo there were lightweight, middleweight, heavyweight and open (any weight) categories. Japan took three gold medals, but Geesink held down Kaminaga to win the open. Since Geesink's retirement the outstanding non-Japanese competitor has been another huge Dutchman, Willem Ruska. He won world heavyweight gold medals in 1967 and 1971, then — the climax of his career — took the heavyweight and open gold medals at the 1972 Munich Olympic Games.

Japan's superiority has been seriously challenged in recent years, from Russia, France, Holland, West Germany and Britain. But the talent in depth in Japan, with some eight million judo players (*judoka*), will keep them ahead for some time yet. The rest of the world, apart perhaps from Russia, is forced to rely on the efforts of exceptional individuals. Top contests are now fought in six categories: lightweight, light-middle-weight, middleweight, light-heavy-weight, heavyweight and the open.

The object of a judo contest is to score a full point (*ippon*) which automatically ends the contest. This can be done by throwing one's opponent flat on his back, holding him down for thirty seconds, or forcing him to submit to an armlock or strangle (the latter techniques cannot be used by judoka under sixteen). A near point (*waza-ari*) is scored if the throw is not perfect or if a hold-down is broken after twenty-five seconds. Two lesser scores, *yuko* and *koka,* are used in high-level contests.

Judo grades are in two categories, *kyu* (pupil) or *Dan* (master) and are illustrated by the colour of belt worn to hold together the judo suit. Progress up the grades is made by defeating opponents at super-vised grading examinations which pro-vide judoka with their first taste of contest.

Judo

The adult beginner wears a white or red belt and the grades then progress thus:

9th kyu   yellow belt
8th kyu   orange belt
7th kyu   orange belt
6th kyu   green belt
5th kyu   green belt
4th kyu   blue belt
3rd kyu   blue belt
2nd kyu   brown belt
1st kyu   brown belt
1st dan   black belt.

A black belt is then worn until 6th Dan when a red-and-white belt can be used on ceremonial occasions. The highest grade ever awarded is 10th Dan, signified by a red belt, but in theory it is possible to have a 12th Dan with a white belt. Dr Kano explained that this completed the full circle of judo knowledge, back to the colour worn by the beginner.

The same sequence of coloured belts is used to indicate the progress of junior *judoka*. However, there are three separate grades, or *mon*, for each colour, indicated by one, two, or three tags sewn to the belt. Thus the first step up the ladder for a young *judoka* is to 1st *mon*, a white belt with one tag. The top junior grade is 18th *mon*, a brown belt with three tags.

A top-level contest begins with the referee and two judges walking on to the mat and bowing to the guests of honour at the event. The judges then bow to the referee before taking their seats at opposite corners of the mat. The fighters come on to the mat from opposite sides and walk towards each other until they are about ten feet apart. They bow to each other and await the referee's instruction to begin. In all matters appertaining to judo the language used is Japanese and it is essential that you learn enough to know what is going on in your own and other contests. Here is a glossary of words which will be useful in your judo career.

Dojo — the hall where judo is practised
Judogi — judo suit
Randori — free practice
Hajime — begin
Matte — break
Yoshi — continue
Sore-made — stop, end of contest
Sono-mama — don't move
Ippon — full point
Waza-ari — near point
Yuko — near *waza-ari*
Koka — near *yuko*.

If a second *waza-ari* is scored by the same contestant this equals *ippon* and two *waza-ari*'s scored in the same contest automatically ends it. The referee will shout '*Waza-ari-awasete ippon*'. If one contestant is holding another down, the referee shouts '*Osae-komi*' and if the hold is broken. '*Toketa*'. Penalties are awarded in top contests, usually for non-combativity or stepping out of the contest area. In order of seriousness they are:

Shido — note
Chui — caution
Keikoku — warning
Hansoku-make — disqualification.

CHAPTER ONE

Breakfalls *(ukemi)*

Before you learn to throw, you must first learn how to fall on the judo mat (*tatami*) without hurting yourself. This soon becomes instinctive, especially for youngsters, and the key points to remember are (*i*) relax, (*ii*) keep your head tucked in and (*iii*) absorb the force of your landing with your arms and feet.

Beginners must become familiar with the surface of the mat so I start by getting them to curl up in a ball and roll smoothly around with no sharp edges like elbows sticking out. This is what Jeremy is doing in picture 1. The next stage is to beat the mat with the arm, palms down, to simulate the shock of landing (2–4).

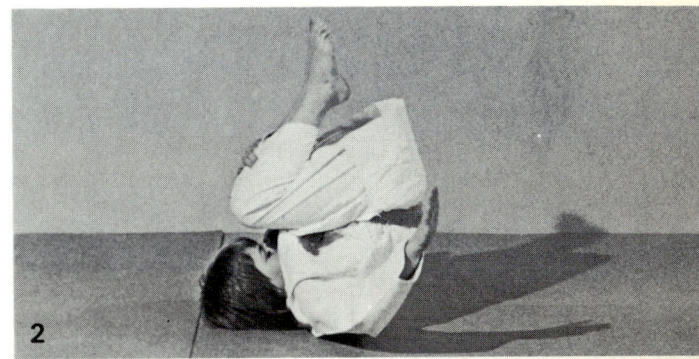

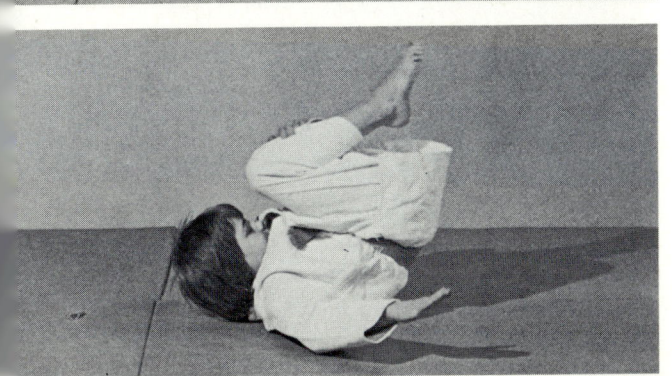

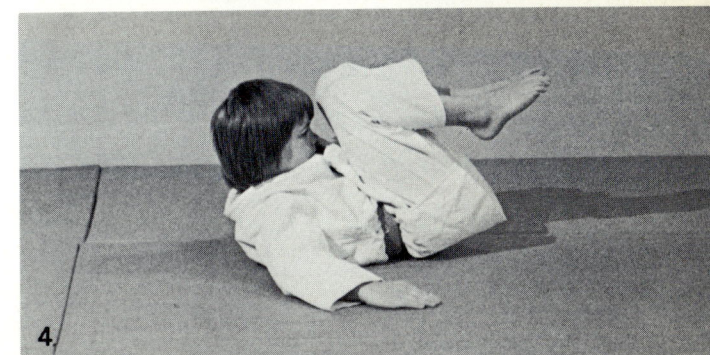

Judo

Pictures 5–8 show how, with the aid of a training partner, you can hit the mat with some impetus without actually being thrown from a standing position. In this way you can gradually build up your confidence. You can see I am holding Jeremy's left wrist and that his left arm is across his chest. I pull smoothly at the wrist and he turns over on his back to breakfall with his right arm. It is important to learn to breakfall with the same facility on either side as you will be meeting both left- and right-handed opponents.

The rolling breakfall (9–12) is more spectacular but is easily mastered and often used in the warm-up sessions which precede a judo practice. Jeremy is rolling over his outstretched arms, keeping his chin down on his chest, and finishing by hitting the mat with his left arm. Remember to keep the body in a smooth, curved or ball shape. When the beginner has gained proficiency in falling he can try the spinroll (13–16), launching himself forward off one foot without the hands touching the ground, rotating in the air and breakfalling largely with the legs. You'll be surprised how easy it is!

5

6

7

8

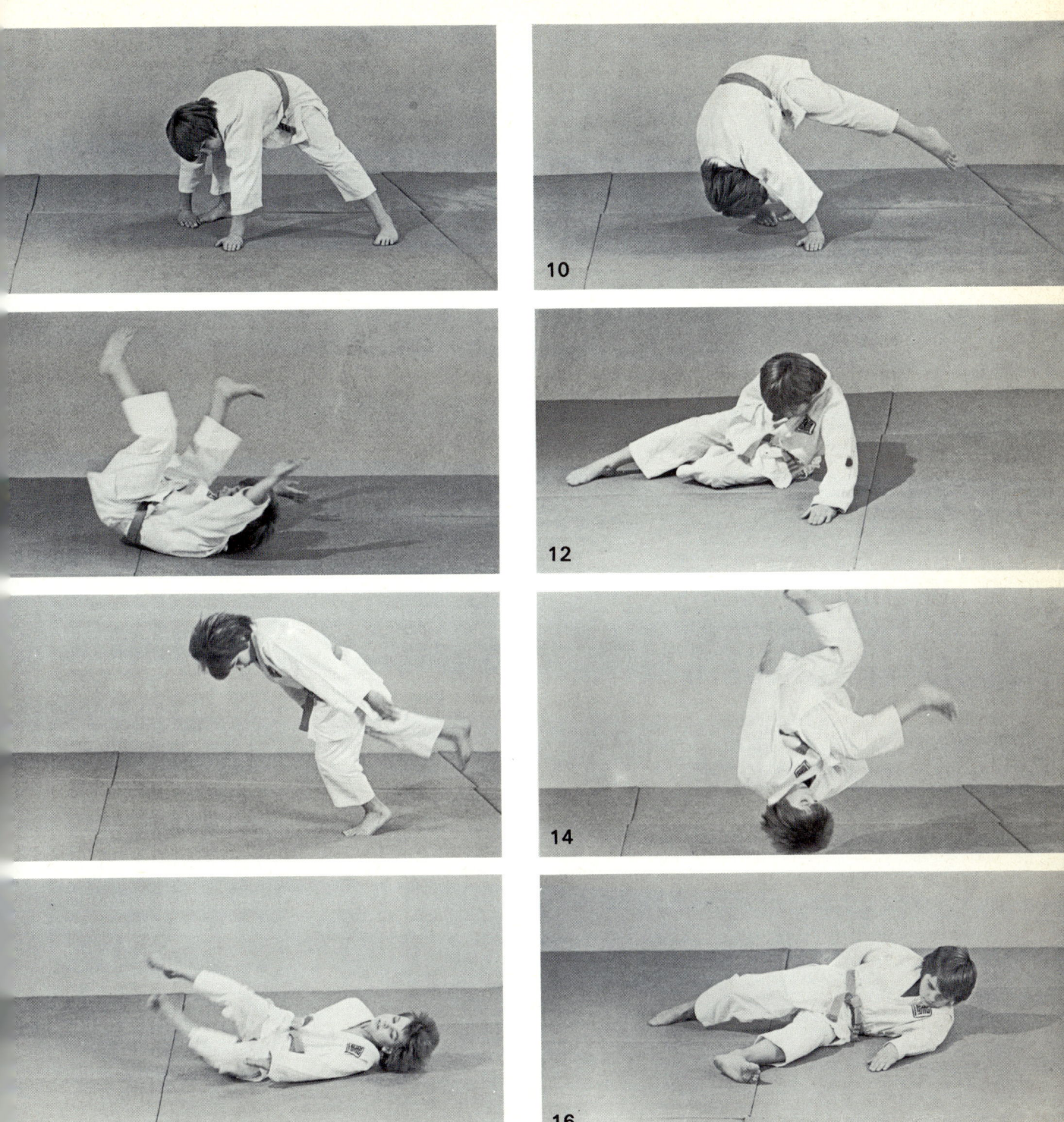

CHAPTER TWO

Balance

Understanding balance, your own and your opponent's, is essential for good judo. The most effective way to throw your partner is to break his balance, then apply the technique where his posture is weak. The throwing actions in this book are based on the fact that however a judoka stands he is always weak in two directions, one directly opposite to the other. Therefore if my initial attack is resisted I must quickly reverse the direction of the attack. This point will be made repeatedly in the following pages. In picture 17 Jeremy is demonstrating my weakness directly forwards, in 18 he shows my weakness directly backwards and in 19 I am breaking his balance to his right-hand side, shown with arrows.

17

18

19

As well as breaking your opponent's balance, you must apply your throwing techniques below his centre of gravity. This obviously varies according to the size of the person and you should adjust the level of your attacks accordingly. Picture 20 shows the small man on the right holding the white belt at his centre of gravity. Notice how different this is from

21

the medium-sized man next to him and the big man on the left. Picture 21 shows the medium-sized man applying a shoulder throw technique well under the big man's centre of gravity and lifting him easily. In picture 22 the big man is trying a similar technique and finding it very difficult. Notice the amount of knee bend needed compared with the previous photograph. In the final picture (23) the big man is using a throw better suited to his build and is lifting his smaller opponent easily by applying the sweeping leg below the centre of gravity.

There is a rough distinction between the small man's techniques and those of the big man. Generally, a small man throws where the hips are used as a

22

fulcrum while a big man throws with a sweeping leg acting as a fulcrum. Examples are *harai-goshi* (23) or *uchi-mata*, shown in the next chapter. However I must emphasise that there is no hard-

Judo

23

and-fast rule on this. For example, Ray Neenan, winner of the lightweight category in the 1975 British Trials, is very tall for a lightweight but has developed a dropping shoulder throw which he often brings off on shorter opponents. I too remember using small man's judo on a much smaller man with success. I threw the brilliant lightweight George Glass, four times British champion, with a shoulder throw during a match at the Albert Hall. Of course, if your opponent is the same size you can use any technique.

CHAPTER THREE

Combinations with Uchi-mata

Inner Thigh Throw (*uchi-mata*)
This powerful throw is my own favourite
and statistics show it is the highest
scoring technique in top-level contests.
One of my most spectacular successes
with it, illustrated below, was against
West German middleweight Gerd Egger
in a 1972 Pre-Olympic International. I
perform *uchi-mata* on the left, and the
other four techniques in this chapter will
be from this same starting point, utilising
my opponent's reaction to the initial
attack. In all the pictures the attacker
(*tori*) wears the white judogi, the
defender (*uke*) the grey judogi.

As you can see in picture 24 I grip the
tip of my brother Shayne's left sleeve with
my right hand while, with my left hand, I
hold at the back of his neck. I draw him
down with both hands and when he
resists upwards I come in for the throw.
Pivoting on the ball of my right foot, I
twist my left leg between Shayne's legs,

*My uchi-mata against West Germany's
Gerd Egger in a 1972 pre-Olympic
international*

Judo

then turn and hop back, (25 and 26).
This action should then move smoothly
into the throwing stage with me driving
my head towards the mat and sweeping
up with my left leg between my opponent's
legs, lifting him high into the air and
dropping him flat on his back for a full
point (27–29). I don't aim to sweep at any
particular point but throw myself forward

as deeply as possible and try to sweep
directly under his centre of gravity while
driving my head down towards the mat,
at the same time turning to the right. To
ensure that my opponent does not twist
on to one shoulder (I discuss this in a later
chapter) and save the full point, I make
my left hand into a fist and drive it to the
mat so as to control his shoulders.

24

25

26

27

28

29

You will not succeed with *uchi-mata* if your entry is timid. When I attack my only thought is to throw myself in as hard, fast and deep as I can, not worrying about what might happen if I miss. It is also worth bearing in mind that your throw is much more likely to be countered if it is half-hearted.

You will find that opponents, whether at club or international level, soon work out ways of making it difficult for you to score with your favourite techniques. The only way to overcome this is constantly to develop your judo and work out new attacks from the initial block. The next sequence of pictures shows one way of overcoming resistance to an *uchi-mata* attack of the kind I have just described. The throw moved into is the stomach wheel (*sumigaeshi*), a sacrifice technique. This term means that I sacrifice my own balance by throwing myself to the mat in order to throw my opponent. I would use such throws primarily to gain a good position to attack on the ground, but these techniques can score, as you can see from the contest picture taken during the 1974 European Championships at Crystal Palace.

Sumigaeshi attack during the 1974 European Championships at Crystal Palace

In picture 30 Andy is attacking Martin with left *uchi-mata*. The attempt is blocked, and as soon as he feels this, he switches to the *sumigaeshi*, completely reversing the direction of attack. He turns his body sharply to the left, pulls strongly with his left hand and presses the top of his left foot on the inside of Martin's right thigh (31). These actions lead into a backwards roll which gives great power to the throwing action (32–33). During the throw, you must pull in very tightly with the left arm, push hard with the right leg and push the left foot strongly into uke's thigh. In pictures 34–35 you can see Andy has made sure of a full point by rolling into a hold-down, the cross body hold (*tate-shio-gatame*). He is astride his

partner's chest, and having maintained control of uke's left sleeve throughout the throw, can get a very strong hold by pressing the sleeve across the side of uke's head and holding it there with his own head.

In the next sequence the attacker, Danny, has come in for left *uchi-mata* only to find the defender, Martin, has prevented him getting in sufficiently deep (36). Danny immediately changes to the major inner reaping throw (*ouchi-gari*). He leaves his right foot as it was for the *uchi-mata* attack (37–38) and hooks his left leg behind Martin's right leg. To execute the throw, he sweeps back with his left leg, at the same time pushing hard in the direction of Martin's right back

42

43

44

corner. When using this throw I always follow uke down to the mat and pin him firmly on his back, preparing to move into a hold-down if *ippon* is not called.

It is vital to remember that you are attacking your opponent's right-rear corner — *not directly* to his rear. The attack is directly opposite to the direction of the *uchi-mata* which started the move and uses the opening created by uke's defence. The action of the head, the heaviest part of the body, is important here, as in all throws. The head movement must be correct before the rest of the body

can follow it into the throw. In pictures 36–39 you can see how Danny has changed the position of his head from looking forward prior to the *uchi-mata* drive to driving back to the right rear for the *ouchi-gari*. The action of the arms in driving the defender back is also vital if a full point is to be scored.

Pictures 40 and 41 show the beginning of another *uchi-mata* attack. This has been stopped by the defender advancing and bracing his left thigh against the attacker's left leg and preventing him completing his turn and starting the upward sweep. The answer for the thwarted attacker, Martin, is to change the direction of his effort and use a throw called minor inner reaping (*kouchi-gari*). To do this, he changes his pull into a push, puts the sole of his left foot behind the defender, Danny's, left ankle and sweeps forward, driving powerfully off his supporting right leg (42–43). In 44 you can see he has gone to the ground with Danny to ensure the point. Again the changing direction of the head is vital as is the punching action of the left fist, directly to uke's rear. This can be clearly seen in pictures 41 and 44.

The minor inner reaping is not one of judo's high scoring 'big throws'. It is classified as a minor technique and is normally used as part of a combination attack. However, I know to my cost that it can be effective. It is the favourite throw (*tokui-waza*) of Shinobu Sekine, the Japanese who won the middleweight gold medal at the Munich Olympics in 1972. He defeated me in the Olympic semi-final after knocking me down several times with *kouchi-gari* and gaining a superiority decision.

An indication of the power that can be put into the technique is shown in the picture below, where my club mate British heavyweight Angelo Parisi, who won an Olympic bronze medal at the age of nineteen, attacks France's Remi Berthet with *kouchi-gari* at the 1975

European Championships in Lyons. Berthet has defended by lifting his foot.

The last three sequences of pictures have shown genuine attacks with *uchi-mata* which failed and were then followed by other throws which took advantage of the defender's reaction. But in the next move I aim to anticipate the defender's evasive action to my *uchi-mata* and throw him with the minor outer hook (*ko-soto-gake*). The opportunity would arise if I had several *uchi-mata* attacks blocked by my opponent pushing his right foot forward, turning his shoulders to the left and pushing me with his right arm (45). This defence is very strong and an opponent would tend to use it every time he was attacked in this way.

To overcome his resistance I make an explosive feint for *uchi-mata* (45) then

45

Britain's Angelo Parisi attacking Remi-Berthet, of France, with kouchi-gari

switch to the attack shown in pictures 46–49. I sink my body below Shayne's straight right arm and hurl myself down behind him, sweeping both his legs away with my left leg. You can see my left arm is over Shayne's right arm throughout and this enables me to exert considerable downward pressure, pushing him towards the mat. With this technique it is very important that the initial feint should be convincing and that the subsequent *ko-soto-gake* be performed quickly and with total abandon. In the picture opposite I am scoring with this throw at the British Open Championships in 1969.

One of the best exponents of *ko-soto-gake* is British middleweight Roy Inman, who also feints before moving into the throw. This move, known to judomen as 'Roy's twitch', is very effective and I have seen him throw many top fighters in international matches in the opening seconds of the bout. In the second picture below Roy is throwing the Japanese 1972 Olympic silver medallist Chiaki Ishii with his 'twitch'.

I am scoring in the British Champion-ships, 1969, with ko-soto-gake

'The Twitch', by Britain's Roy Inman

CHAPTER FOUR

Front and Back Throws

The Body Drop Throw (tai-otoshi)
As mentioned earlier, this was my favourite throw in the early stages of my career. I had to stop using it so frequently after I broke my wrist in the final of the 1970 European Championships and found I no longer had sufficient wrist power to bring it off against strong opponents.

I perform *tai-otoshi* on the right. As you see in the first picture (50) I grip with my right hand on Shayne's loose left lapel while with my left hand I hold the end of

Shayne's right sleeve. With the left hand I hold over the defender's right arm so I can exert pressure on it (51). This prevents him stopping the throw by putting his right hand on the mat. Starting with my right foot forward I pivot on this foot and take my left foot round outside Shayne's left foot (51—53). While doing this I extend my body upwards — you can see I am on my toes in picture 52 — and try to draw my opponent up and forward using the rising movement of my body rather

54

55

than just arm strength. I then very swiftly drop down in front of the defender with both knees bent and my right leg wrapped around the defender's shin (53). I bring off the throw by straightening both legs very quickly, springing my opponent into the air (54) and simultaneously pull down and around to my left with both hands (55).

Notice how I keep looking at Shayne until I move into the throwing position in picture 53. Throwing the head forward and to the left then gives added power. I also emphasise the rising and dropping movements. These two actions must be smooth and continuous with the pull on the defender maintained throughout. The left hand action starts as an upward, outward pull and concludes with a downward pull. I aim to have my right forearm pressed against the defender's left chest

with the palm side of my clenched right fist against the left side of the defender's head. The final important point is the springing off both legs which launches my opponent into the air.

In my opinion the best *tai-otoshi* in the world is that of my friend and British team mate Dave Starbrook, the light-heavy-weight silver medallist at the Munich Olympics. Dave's *tai-otoshi* is so powerful, he sometimes stuns his opponents with the speed he crashes them over. Just as I use *sumigaeshi* as an opposite direction attack with *uchi-mata* (see Chapter 3) so Dave uses it with his *tai-otoshi* when his opponents defend back against it. An example of Dave's ability is shown over-leaf where he triumphantly throws one of his bitterest rivals, Yugoslavia's Goran Zuvela, for *waza-ari* in the 1975 European Championships.

25

Taiotoshi by Dave Starbrook, of Britain, against Yugoslavia's Goran Zuvela

The Shoulder Drop (seoi-otoshi)

Pictures 56 to 61 illustrate another power-ful right-handed technique, the shoulder drop (*seoi-otoshi*) which bears some resemblance to the body drop. You can see that in picture 56 the defender,

Martin, has his left foot forward and right foot back, indicating that his balance is weak towards his right-hand corner. The attacker, Danny, takes advantage of this by making a feint with his right leg (56), then places his foot extended at the

outside of Martin's right foot (57), his right knee is slightly bent. He ensures that his right elbow is thrust up tight under the defender's right armpit and he is looking at the mat (58) near his left foot. Two things are now clear. The attacker's head has turned three-quarters of a circle from the starting position and the left hand is pulling strongly around to where he is looking.

In picture 59 you see the beginning of the bend in Danny's body, and right leg, emphasising that the turn of the head is all-important in judo throws. The next picture (60) is probably the most important as it shows the inside of the attacker's knee springing back and lifting the defender into the air. The attacker is also turning his body as much as possible. The defender is seen at the top of his flight in picture 60 with the attacker's right leg and foot fully stretched to derive maximum spring. In the final picture (61), Danny, to ensure that Martin lands flat on his back, has collapsed his right leg and landed on top of him.

Some of the best *seoi-otoshis* I have seen performed have come from Angelo Parisi, who combines his natural power and speed to make it quite devastating. Here we illustrate Angelo at work in the 1974 European Championships.

Angelo Parisi in the 1974 European Championships

Minor Inner Reaping *(kouchi-gari)*

Picture 62 opposite shows a special form of the *kouchi-gari* (minor inner reaping) illustrated in the first chapter. I use this when an opponent has defended against my *tai-otoshi*. In this picture the attacker, Martin, has a normal right-side grip with his left hand, gripping the defender, Danny's, sleeve. But notice how, unlike the previous throw, the defender has advanced his right foot. It would be very difficult to throw him with *tai-otoshi* in this position as most of his weight is on the right foot.

The trick is to push the defender backwards (63) while faking a *tai-otoshi*-type movement with the left leg. When he defends against the push you can see Martin has taken a long step forward with his right foot, placed it against Danny's right foot and quickly caught Danny's right ankle with his left hand just as he begins to step backwards with the right foot (63–64). Martin drives his shoulder down, presses Danny's head back with his right hand and pushes hard off his left leg (64–65–66). It is important that the attacker keeps his body straight during the main part of the throwing action and that his head drives in very low. In picture 67 I am showing Martin the catching action, the left hand holding the ankle, very close to the foot.

62

63

64

65

66

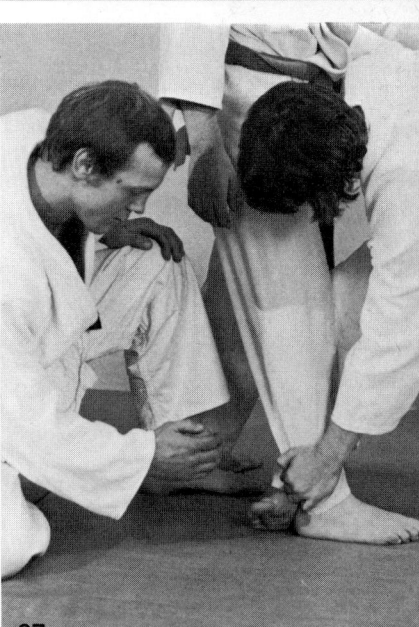

67

29

Judo

Major Outer Reaping *(o-soto-gari)*
Another throw I perform from this same right hand position is the major outer reaping *(o-soto-gari)*, a powerful technique used by many leading internationals. The form shown here could be described as a double-barrelled *o-soto-gari* giving, as it does, the attacker a second chance after his initial effort has failed. Picture 68 shows the same starting position as for the last sequence. The defender's right foot is forward, therefore he is weak diagonally to the right front corner and left rear of the picture. This time we will attack to the rear.

The attacker, Andy, must concentrate all his power through his left arm down towards the mat, trying to pin the defender's weight on his right foot. In picture 69 you can see that, having done this, Andy has also brought his right leg through and hooked the heel behind

Martin's knee. The attacker now starts to push back viciously with his right hand and takes a gigantic hop forward with the left foot. But in 70 you can see that Martin has stopped the throw by pushing forward strongly with his right leg and he is now in a strong position leaning on Andy.

Now begins the second stage of the attack. The attacker throws the heaviest part of his body (his head) forward and pulls hard with his left hand, wrapping uke's arm around his abdomen (I am pointing this out in picture 70). Andy now takes a smaller step towards his opponent's weak rear corner, sweeping backwards strongly against the defender's right leg, with the left hand pushing backwards and the knuckles of the right hand pushing against the defender's collar bone, pictures 71 and 72.

Looking at 72 you will notice three

68

69

70

main points: (i) The attacker's right hand has followed his opponent to the mat ensuring that he lands squarely on his back; (ii) Andy is up on the ball of his left foot securing maximum height throughout the throwing movement; (iii) A point I regard as of paramount importance, the right sweeping foot is still driving back even when the defender has hit the mat.

You can compare this position, head towards the mat and leg in the air, with that of a see-saw. When one end goes down the other comes up. In this throw if the toes of the sweeping leg are slightly more pointed than in the picture this ensures maximum reach and power. These points apply to any throw where there is a sweeping movement. Try to keep the see-saw action in mind when practising these throws. Remember that the sweeping leg should be the last part of your body to touch the mat.

Two British international lightweights, Ray Neenan and Dave Lawrence, use the type of *o-soto-gari* I have described. Both have long legs which gives them a reach advantage when hooking in behind the opponent's knee, but you don't need long legs to make it work and I use it frequently in conjunction with other throws.

71

72

CHAPTER FIVE

'The Switch'

The Shoulder Throw *(ippon seoi-nage)*
The throws performed in this chapter, of which the shoulder throw is the main one, are all performed from the same opening gambit which I call 'the switch'. The opponent is led to expect an attack from the right only to be surprised when you spin in on his left. The form of shoulder throw shown here is used a great deal by myself and has become very popular in major competitions.

In the first picture (73) you see Jeremy has a right-handed grip with his left hand holding either his partner's right sleeve at the tip or clasping his opponent's wrist between forefinger and thumb, so preventing him holding with his right hand. Jeremy's right foot is forward as if he might attack in that direction. But in picture 74 he has jumped in the air and started to rotate the other way, attacking Andy's left front corner. In picture 75 you can see that while in mid-air he is bringing his left hand through with the turn of the body and is starting to bend his knees prior to landing on them between Andy's

legs, (76). The left hand at this stage is wrapped tightly around his opponent's left upper arm with the bicep thrust into his armpit.

In picture 78 I am pointing out the exact position of the attacker's body just prior to the throw. The most important point is that the toes be well tucked in and that the left arm be wrapped tight around uke's left arm with the right hand pulling down towards the mat. I find a lot of people fear they will hurt their knees when they jump in for this throw. Just try to think of it as a form of breakfall with the weight taken evenly on the knees and the tucked-in toes. After a while the movement becomes effortless.

76

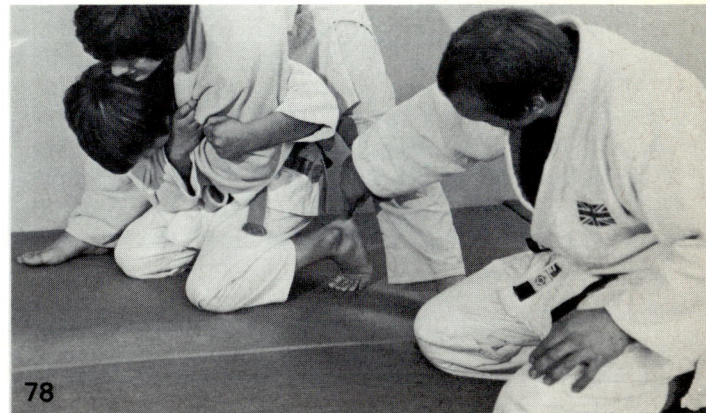

78

To achieve the actual throw from pictures 76 and 77 you straighten your body, with the power coming from the toes and knees, at the same time driving forward and turning to the right. In picture 77 Jeremy is lying in the extended position with the weight of his shoulder on his opponent's left hand side.

This turning and straightening is vividly illustrated by the contest pictures where I am throwing French middle-

weight Jean-Paul Coche, like myself twice European Champion, at the 1975 European Championships. Unfortunately, the referee was the only person in the stadium at Lyons who did not see the throw and I was awarded no score. Some judo fighters have been using a half-hearted version of this throw as a defensive, time-wasting device, usually if they are ahead in a contest and just waiting for time to be called. The European Judo

33

Throwing Jean-Paul Coche, of France, with ippon seoi-nage

Union has now decided to penalise this. Fighters are also not allowed to grab the opponent's leg directly after such an attack.

Gripping

I include this sequence to show the importance of gripping. With the correct grip you can dominate your opponent, preventing him throwing you while setting him up for your own pet technique. I regard the correct grip as contributing twenty-five per cent to the success of a throw. Non-judoka watching top-level contests are probably puzzled and bored by the sight of two men constantly breaking one another's grip on the jackets, often for minutes on end. The reason is that once people of this calibre have their grip, a strong attack is not far behind.

The orthodox right-handed hold is with the left hand gripping the opponent's right sleeve near the elbow and the right hand on the opponent's left lapel. But as we have already seen, there is a variety of other grips. It is even permitted to grab the belt to make a throw and Russian judoka are particularly adept at this move which is widely used in their native Sambo wrestling.

A fighter's favourite grip can also be a give-away for the throw he is about to attempt, so it is vital that you learn how to fool the opposition. You don't necessarily have to be able to throw on either side, although this is an obvious advantage. As I showed with my switch techniques, it is often enough to make your opponent believe you are going to throw on one side and then come in on the other. I always make a point when starting with a right-hand grip, as Jeremy is in this sequence (79), to attack strongly on that side so as to build up a reflex defence from my opponent.

Assuming that Jeremy has implanted the expectation of attacks from that side in his opponent's mind, you can see that in picture 80 he has taken his right hand off the jacket, pulling it towards him and

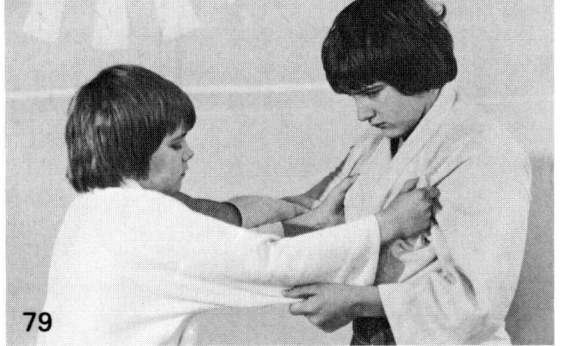

79

80

81

82

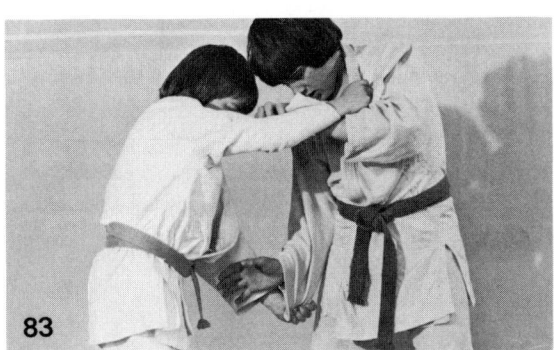

83

84

making a circular anti-clockwise movement in order to go under his opponent's left arm. In picture 81 you can see he next quickly grabs his opponent's left lapel with his left hand. This is a very risky part of the move, for tori, the attacker, has for a split second neither hand gripping his opponent. That is why it must be performed fast.

In fact I find opponents are generally so baffled with the gripping change that they don't take advantage of this instance when you have no control of them at all. In picture 81 Jeremy is feeding his partner's left-hand lapel into his own right hand, and in 82 and 83 has taken his left hand back as if to grip his partner's right sleeve. From this position he swings his right leg backwards as if trying to catch up with his left hand as it comes across his partner's body toward his left hand side. He pushes his left hand under the left armpit of his opponent into position for the shoulder throw (84). It is a great advantage to pin your opponents left arm between your right forearm and left biceps. This ensures that he cannot pull back with the left arm during the throw.

The preparation for this particular grip is vividly illustrated in the contest picture where Ray Neenan is about to attack an opponent in the 1974 European Championships with a low shoulder throw.

Britain's Ray Neenan, right, in the 1974 European Championships

The Lift Pull Hip Throw

(tsuri-komi-goshi)

Another throw I go into from the switch is the lift pull hip throw (*tsuri-komi-goshi*). I grip both sides of Shayne's jacket between the lapel and armpit, gathering the loose cloth and hooking my hands well in. The work of the arms is particularly important in this throw, which is used by a number of leading fighters, including my Budokwai clubmate Tony Sweeney, the heavyweight in the 1964 British team at the Tokyo Olympics.

Initially, I like to get as far away from my opponent as possible. To start the feint to the right, I take a big step with my right foot towards his right foot (85) ensuring that I keep on the ball of that foot. At the same time I try to make an upward movement with my elbows which opens Shayne up to a weak position in his left front corner. I generally find that my opponent defends against this by a slight bend of the right knee as he is anticipating that my attack will be on that side. In picture 86 you can see I start to bring my left foot through from that back position between my body and Shayne's as if to attempt *uchi-mata*. But, keeping my arms in the bent position with the elbows well up, I bring my left foot through, as you can see in picture 87, and place it some

86

87

89

90

distance away from my opponent's left foot. This ensures there is a gap between our bodies, leaving me room to change the technique if my opponent should change his defence.

You can see from the same photograph that I am on the balls of both feet, my head is still looking at Shayne and my hips are slightly forward of the top of my body. I now whirl into the throwing movement,

37

Judo

bringing my left elbow down and smashing my left forearm against Shayne's right chest. In picture 88 I have brought my left hip right through, keeping my body bent with the trunk sideways at a 90 degree angle which ensures that Shayne is sprung over my extended left hip.

By this time my left elbow has pushed hard and high up under Shayne's armpit and I am pulling and turning towards my own right knee. In pictures 89 and 90 I force my opponent over my hip with my left hand while pulling with my right hand and springing up on to my toes. Again I ensure the full point by punching my opponent's shoulders into the mat with my left hand in picture 90.

corner, as you can see in picture 91. This move, combined with a pull to the left with my left hand, causes Shayne to resist to his right front corner. In picture 92 I have changed the direction of my attack, spinning on the ball of my right foot while maintaining a steady pull with my bent arms. In pictures 91 and 92 my right arm is pulling Shayne's left arm upwards and outwards while my leg swings through and my body falls away from that of my opponent. I particularly try to drive my left leg between my partner's left knee and left hip. It is very important that, as the leg sweeps through, I pull Shayne towards me as well as leaning away and keeping my body rigid, as in picture 93. Momentum

91 92 93

The Major Wheel Throw (o-guruma)
The major wheel throw (o-guruma) is the third technique from the switch. Again I take a double lapel grip and feint with my right foot, this time to the left front

is very important for this throw and it is initially created by my rapid spin on the ball of my right foot. It is maintained by sweeping my left leg through the gap between the two bodies as fast as possible

94

95

(91—94). In picture 94 you can see I am balanced on the ball of my right foot and my body is in a rigid position. The end of the throw comes from the turn of the top half of my body, wheeling my opponent over my leg (95).

This is without doubt the most difficult throw in judo to execute properly, but it remains one of my favourites because of the sheer beauty of the entire movement. Although it is not one of my main contest techniques I have thrown a lot of people with it. The example here is from the semi-final of the African Games in Pretoria, seen from the rear view.

O-guruma, during semi-final of African Games in Pretoria

39

CHAPTER SIX

Avoidance Tactics

Every judoka should work at twisting out of throws, thus avoiding landing flat on the back and losing by *ippon*. I spend a quarter of my training sessions working at avoidance techniques and recommend all judoka to develop their spatial awareness. I might mention that throughout my thirteen years of top-level judo I have only been thrown for *ippon* twice. As I must have had over 2,000 individual contests in this time I think the value of this type of training is obvious. To develop these cat-like movements I recommend gymnastics and, best of all, twisting movements on a trampoline.

In the five pictures taken at the 1975 European Championships (96–100) David Finch has expertly captured me twisting out of a very powerful throwing attempt by Yugoslavia's Obadov. If you look at the clock in the background, showing how much remains of the six-

96

97

98

99

100

minute contest, you can see that all this
movement took place in just one second.
In the first picture I have been picked up
with a shoulder wheel throw (*kata-
guruma*). Obadov's intention is to throw
me down on my back, but I have other
ideas. Notice the clock in photos 96–97
– 2.24. In this position I find it very
important to look exactly where I am
going to fall, even if this means contorting
my body. In picture 98, I start to bring my
right hand through as if to reach for the
floor. My legs are still in more or less the
same position as when I was picked up
but the top half of my body is beginning a
very strenuous turn. A close examination
of the clock in 98 will show the change
from 2.24 to 2.23 still in progress.

In picture 99 I have managed to get my
left hand to the ground with the whole of
my body passing where I was originally
looking and the bottom half of my body
turning the opposite way. My right leg is

*Inverted twist, avoiding a throw from Russia's
Tsupachenko in the 1974 European Championships*

Judo

beginning to hit the mat at the same time and on the same side as my left hand, perfectly seen in photo 100. If Obadov in picture 98 had followed me to the ground and fallen with me he would most probably have made a score of ½ point (*wazari*). I call this type of movement the inverted twist.

The other illustration is from the final of The 1974 European Team Championship.

Russian middleweight Tsupachenko has caught me with a *tai-otoshi* technique and I have again gone into an inverted twisting movement. You can see to what extent my body is twisting by looking at my left arm and right foot. To master techniques like these you must work at keeping supple and I recommend that you practise them by asking a partner to throw you on to a gymnastic crash mat.

CHAPTER SEVEN

Groundwork *(ne waza)*

Many people ignore this vital aspect of judo, and do so at their peril! Just as many contests are won on the ground as in stand fighting, so it is obviously important for every judoka to become efficient in the application of hold-downs, armlocks and strangles. Ideally, one's judo should flow easily from standing to groundwork. Frequently you will find that having thrown a partner imperfectly you are in a good position to apply a groundwork technique and score a full point. It is worth bearing in mind that a correctly applied armlock or strangle will bring a rapid submission but a hold-down has to be maintained for thirty seconds. As you have seen in the preceding pages, many throws involve going to the mat with your partner. Once there, it is proficiency in groundwork which will determine the victor.

The Scarf Hold *(kesa-gatame)*
into Strangle *(shime-waza)*
This is a very popular and effective hold-down. As you can see in picture 101 I apply it by lying across my opponent, with my right side on his chest, my elbow flat on his left shoulder and his right arm

101

trapped up under my left armpit. Key points are to keep your weight on your opponent's chest, try to lift his head slightly with your right arm and keep your legs well spread for firm balance. My favourite left-hand hold is under my opponent's right elbow. Dave Starbrook, one of the world's leading groundwork experts, uses a variation of this hold as his main *ne-waza* technique and you can see him clamping it on in the contest picture on p. 44. Notice the spread of the legs and how his weight is pressing on to his opponent's chest. You will see that Dave holds his opponent's left wrist with his right hand. This puts him in a good position to apply an armlock if the man

Kesa gatame, by Dave Starbrook

underneath struggles and straightens his arm. One reason Dave is so strong on the ground is that he never loses an opportunity to follow his opponent down and and continue the fight. This is a principle everyone should apply in practice sessions.

In pictures 102–103–104 I am applying a strangle from the scarf hold. The opponent submits to this by tapping me twice. Remember, you cannot use

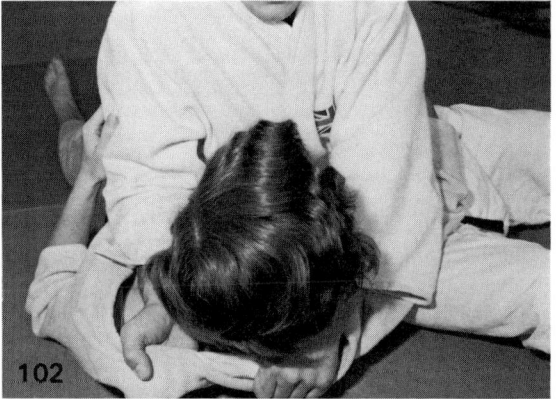

102

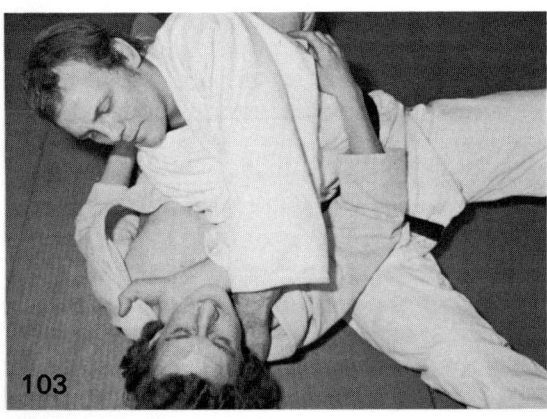

103

104

strangles if you are under sixteen. My first move (101) is to catch his left lapel close under the neck with my palm facing outwards (102). At the same time I keep control of my partner's left hand. Putting steady pressure on my partner's rib cage with my right elbow, I now catch his collar on the right-hand side with my left hand palm downwards (102). In picture 103 you can see I begin to bring my right elbow across my partner's throat, pulling steadily with the left hand to ensure that he does not turn into or away from me and ease the pressure on his throat. I bring my left leg across his head (104) to apply the strangle by pushing with the cutting edge

of the right wrist across the front of his neck while pulling steadily and evenly with the left hand. I have managed to score many times with this particular strangle in competition, one reason being that, just before it is applied, my opponents have believed themselves in a good position to escape.

Cross Body Hold *(tate-shio-gatame)* **into Armlock** *(juji-gatame)*
Picture 105 shows *tate-shio-gatame* which was briefly described in Chapter Three. I always find when applying this hold-down that it is of paramount importance to trap my opponent's left arm

105

106

107

108

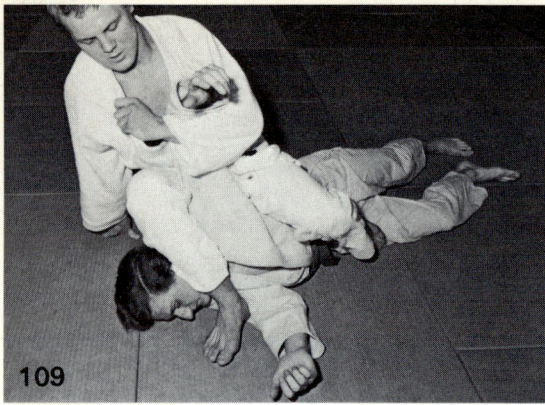

109

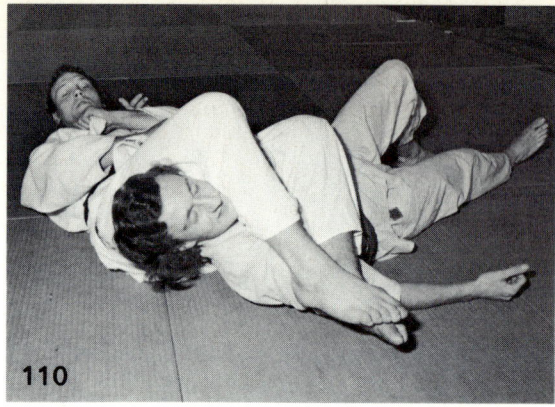

110

so the arm lies along the side of his face. From this position I can apply pressure with my own left arm, just alongside his head, by pushing his head by the side of his triceps and flexing my own biceps. This makes it very uncomfortable for my opponent and dissuades him from struggling. Sometimes he will even submit.

In the five pictures 106–110 I show how to trick an opponent by leading him to believe he can escape from his hold by turning to his right, away from me (106), while in fact I am luring him into an arm-lock. Once he starts to turn, I catch his left arm by hooking my left arm around it. This is shown very clearly in picture 106. When he has almost turned on to his face, I bring my right leg across his neck (107 and 108), at the same time catching my right lapel with my left hand. In picture 109 and 110 I roll backwards, pulling my partner to his original position on his back, keeping good control of his extended arm by ensuring my left-hand grip is very tight. In picture 110 my legs are across his body, the knees gripping closely together making sure he cannot sit up. The lock is applied from this position by raising my hips from the mat. In the contest picture,

taken at the 1974 European Championships, I am about to throw my right leg across the Austrian champion's neck. Notice the tightness of my knee grip just prior to the left leg going across his trunk. In fact he is submitting before the lock is applied owing to the tightness of this knee grip.

I am about to throw my right leg across the Austrian champion's neck

Broken Upper Four Quarters Hold
(kuzure-kami-shio-gatame)

This is the strongest hold-down in my repertoire. In picture 111 Jeremy is kneeling at the top right-hand corner of his opponent between his right ear and his right elbow. This is quite a common position to find oneself in during a contest and I have found that opponents will often try to grab their own lapels with their right arm to prevent me applying the armlock we have just described. In this picture I am pointing under Jeremy's arm explaining that he should now wrap this arm around his opponent's bent right arm, concentrating on trapping the elbow in the bent position and wrapping around it tightly (112). Jeremy applies the hold-down in picture 113 by taking his left hand around the left-hand side of his opponent's neck, and linking his hands together under his opponent's body. From here the hips are pushed towards the mat and the legs spread to ensure the partner cannot move from side to side. In picture 114 I'm pointing to Jeremy's left leg which has the toes tucked well into the mat to ensure a good grip when pushing forward. The two most important points of this powerful holding are the linked hands (113) and the trapping of the opponent's right arm under your arm (112).

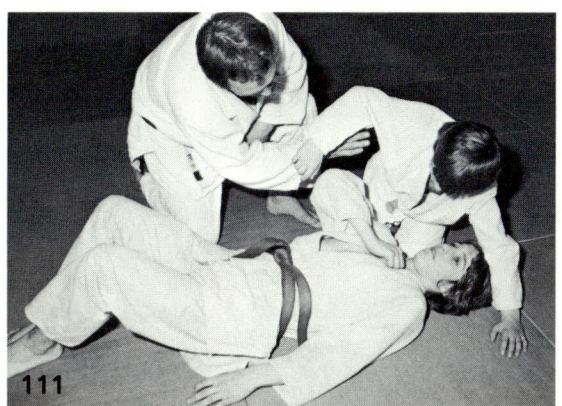

111

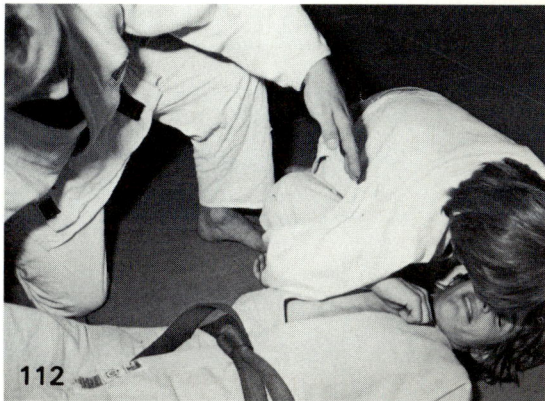

112

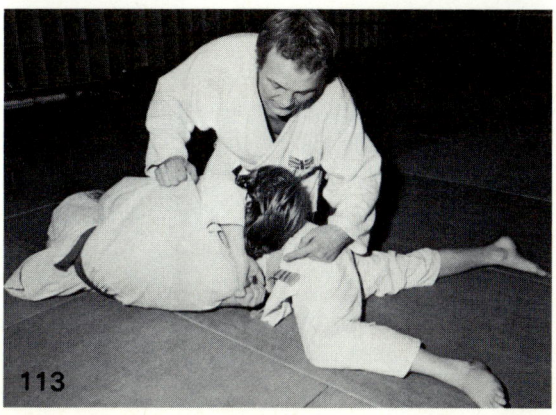

113

114

Brian Jacks's Contest Record

5th Dan of the British Judo Association.

European junior middleweight champion 1964, East Berlin.

Bronze medallist in the lightweight category at the 1964 Senior European Championships, East Berlin.

Lightweight in the 1964 Olympic Games, Tokyo.

European junior middleweight champion 1965, Scheveningen, Holland.

Silver medallist at welterweight in the 1965 Senior European Championships, Madrid.

Silver medallist at middleweight at the 1966 Adriatic Cup Competition, Split, Yugoslavia.

Bronze medallist at middleweight in the 1966 British Open Championships, Crystal Palace.

Bronze medallist at middleweight at the 1967 Junior European Championships, Lisbon.

Bronze medallist at middleweight at the 1967 Senior European Championships, Rome.

Bronze medallist at middleweight at the 1967 World Championships, Salt Lake City, USA.

Open (any weight) champion of Great Britain 1969, Crystal Palace.

European middleweight champion, 1970, East Berlin.

Bronze medallist at middleweight in the 1971 European Championships, Goteborg, Sweden.

Captain of the 1972 British Olympic Judo Team and middleweight bronze medallist, Munich.

European middleweight champion 1973, Madrid.

South African Games middleweight champion 1973, Pretoria.

Bronze medallist at middleweight at the World Student Games 1974, Brussels.

British middleweight champion 1974, Crystal Palace.

Silver medallist at the pre-Olympic Tournament 1975, Montreal.

Entered the British Trials for the past thirteen years and won eleven times.

British Junior Team Manager.

Contest Rules of the International Judo Federation

Article 1. Competition Area

The competition area shall be of a minimum of 14 m × 14 m and a maximum of 16 m × 16 m and shall be covered by tatami or a similarly acceptable material.

The competition area shall be divided into two zones. The demarcation between these two zones shall be called the danger area and shall be indicated by a coloured area, generally red, approximately 1 metre wide forming part of or attached to the mat, parallel to the four sides of the competition area.

The area within and including the coloured area shall be called the contest area and shall be always of a minimum of 9 m × 9 m or a maximum of 10 m × 10 m. The area outside the coloured area shall be called the safety area, and shall never be less than 2 metres 50 cms wide.

The above competition area must be mounted on a resilient platform.

Commentary

Should two or more competition areas be placed on the same resilient platform as mentioned above it is permissible for such adjoining safety areas to utilise mats common to both areas.

Article 2. Costume

The contestants shall wear judogi (judo costume) and generally, as directed, shall also wear a red or white tape or ribbon tied over the regulation belt.

The judogi (judo costume) to be worn by the contestants shall comply with the following conditions:

(a) The jacket shall be long enough to cover the hips and be tied at the waist by the belt.

(b) The sleeves shall be loose and long enough to cover more than half of the forearm (there should be an opening of between 3 and 5 cm between the cuff and the largest part of the forearm).

(c) The trousers shall be loose and long enough to cover more than half of the lower leg (there should be an opening of between 5 and 8 cm between the bottom of the trousers and the largest part of the calf).

Judo

(d) The belt shall be tied with a square knot tight enough to prevent the jacket from being too loose and long enough to go twice round the body and leave about 15 cm protruding from each side of the knot when tied.

Commentary

If the judogi of a contestant does not comply with this article the referee must order the contestant to change in the shortest possible time into a judogi which does comply with the article.

Although not stated in the article the referee should also ensure that the judogi is uncoloured, i.e. white or off-white.

Article 3. Personal Requirements

The contestants shall keep their nails cut short and shall not wear any metallic articles which may possibly injure or endanger the opponent.

Commentary

The phrase 'metallic articles' includes all 'hard objects' which may cause injury.

The referee should also ensure that the personal hygiene of both contestants is of a high standard. For example should a contestant arrive on the mat with dirty feet he must be told to wash them and anyone wearing a dirty judogi must be made to change it.

Article 4. Location

The contest shall be fought in the contest area. However any technique applied when one or both of the contestants is outside the contest area shall not be recognised. That is to say that if one contestant shall have even one of his feet outside the contest area while standing or more than half of his body outside the contest area whilst doing sutemi-waza (sacrifice throws) or ne-waza (groundwork) he shall be considered as being outside the contest area.

However, where one contestant throws his opponent outside the contest area but himself stays within the contest area long enough for the effectiveness of the technique to be clearly apparent, the technique shall be recognised.

When osaekomi has been called, it may continue — until the time allowed for the osaekomi expires or toketa is called — so long as at least one player has any part of his body touching the contest area (including the danger area).

Commentary

As the coloured danger area which defines the contest area from the safety area is immediately inside the boundary of the contest area, any contestant whose feet are still touching the coloured danger area in the standing position should be considered as being still within the contest area.

When performing sutemi-waza a throw is considered valid if the thrower has one half or more of his body within the contest area. Therefore neither foot of the thrower should leave the contest area before his back or hips touch the mat.

In ne-waza the action is valid and may continue so long as both contestants have at least half of their bodies inside the contest area.

If the thrower falls outside the contest area whilst making a throw, the action will only

50

be considered for point scoring purposes where the opponent's body touches the mat before the thrower's. Therefore if a thrower's knee, hand or any other part of his body touches the ground before his opponent's any result obtained thereby should be disregarded.

If, however, during the course of an attack such as o-uchi-gari or ko-uchi-gari the foot or leg of the thrower leaves the contest area and moves over the mats of the safety area the action should be considered valid for point scoring purposes so long as the thrower does not place any weight upon the foot or leg while it is out of the contest area.

Article 5. Position at Start of Contest
The contestants shall stand facing each other at the centre of the contest area and approximately 4 m apart and shall make a standing bow.

The contest shall begin immediately after the announcement of hajime (begin) by the referee and shall always begin with both contestants in the standing position.
No Commentary

Article 6. Start and End of Contest
The referee shall announce hajime (begin) in order to start the contest after the contestants have bowed to each other.

The referee shall announce sore-made (that is all) to end the contest.

At the end of the contest the contestants shall return to the places in which they started the contest and standing facing each other shall again make a standing bow after the referee has indicated the result of the contest.
No Commentary

Article 7. Result
The result of a contest shall be judged only on the basis of nage-waze (throwing techniques) and katame-waza (grappling techniques).
No Commentary

Article 8. Termination by Ippon (full point)
The contest shall immediately end if and when one of the contestants scores ippon (full point).
No Commentary

Article 9. Entry into Ne-waza (groundwork)
The contestants shall be able to change from standing position to ne-waza (groundwork) in the following cases, but should the employment of the technique not be continuous the referee may, at his discretion, order both contestants to resume the standing position.
  (a) When a contestant after obtaining some result by a throwing technique changes without interruption into ne-waza (groundwork) and takes offensive.
  (b) When one of the contestants falls to the ground, following the unsuccessful application of a throwing technique, the other may follow him to the ground or

when one of the contestants is unbalanced and is liable to fall to the ground after the unsuccessful application of a throwing technique the other may take advantage of his opponent's unbalanced position to take him to the ground.

(c) When one contestant obtains some considerable effect by applying a shime-waza (strangle) or kansetsu-waza (a lock) in the standing position and then changes without interruption to ne-waza (groundwork).

(d) When one contestant takes his opponent down into ne-waza (groundwork) by the particularly skilful application of movement which although resembling a throwing technique does not fully qualify as such.

(e) In any other case where one contestant may fall down or be about to fall down not covered by the preceding sub sections of this article the other contestant may take advantage of his opponent's position to go into ne-waza (groundwork).

Commentary

If one contestant tries to apply ju-ji-gatame or any similar technique from the standing position and the result is not immediately apparent, the referee shall call matte.

For further comments see Commentary No. 6 of Article 31.

Article 10. Duration

The duration of the contest shall be arranged in advance and shall be not less than 3 minutes and not more than 20 minutes. This arranged time may however be extended in certain special cases.

No Commentary

Article 11. Time Signal

The end of the time allotted for the contest shall be indicated to the referee by the ringing of a bell or other similar audible method.

No Commentary

Article 12. Technique Coinciding with Time Signal

Any throwing technique which is applied simultaneously with the bell (or other method of indicating the end of the time allotted) shall be recognised and when an osaekomi (holding) is similarly announced simultaneously with the signal bell, etc., the time allotted for the contest shall be extended until either ippon is scored or the referee announces toketa (hold broken).

Further, any technique applied after the ringing of the bell or other device to indicate the expiry of the time of the contest shall not be valid, even if the referee has not at that time called sore-made.

Commentary

Although a throwing technique may be applied simultaneously with the bell, if the referee decides that it will not be effective immediately he should announce sore-made.

Article 13. Sono-mama

In any case where the referee wishes to stop the contest (e.g. in order to adjust the dress of the players, or to address either of them without causing a change in their positions), he will call 'sono-mama'. To recommence the contest, he will call 'yoshi'.

The time between the announcement of sone mama (do not move) and yoshi (carry on) shall be excluded from the specified time for the duration of the contest.

Commentary

Whenever the referee applies the rule and action of sono-mama he must be particularly careful that there is no change of relative positions of both the contestants.

Article 14. Responsibility

All actions and decisions taken in accordance with the majority of three rule as in Article 26 by the referee and judges shall be final and without appeal.

No Commentary

Article 15. Officials

In general the contest shall be conducted by one referee and two judges. However, in certain circumstances it may be permissible to have one referee and one judge or even just one referee.

Commentary

The referee and judges shall be assisted by a contest recorder, who shall visibly record in writing or by means of a suitable apparatus, all scores and penalties announced by the referee, as accepted or modified by the judges under the majority of three rule. At the end of the contest the contest recorder shall, if requested, indicate to the referee and judges the total scores and/or penalties awarded to each contestant.

When recording penalties, the contest recorder must ensure that only one penalty is shown recorded against any one contestant at a time. For example, if one contestant is penalised with a shido and is then given a further penalty of a chui or a keikoku, the earlier lesser offence must always be removed from the score once the new offence has been added.

Article 16. Position and Function of Referee

The referee shall stay generally within the contest area and has the sole responsibility for conducting the contest and administering the judgement.

Commentary

In general and from time to time the referee and judges shall observe that the scores recorded by the contest recorder are correct with the scores that have been announced.

Article 17. Position and Function of Judges

The judges shall assist the referee and shall be positioned opposite each other at two corners outside the contest area.

Commentary

As the judges will be seated on the safety area they must be particularly alert to the need to remove both themselves and their chair should it appear that one or more contestants may leave the contest area at the place where they are sitting.

Article 18. Ippon (full point)

The referee shall announce ippon (full point) when in his opinion a throwing or grappling technique applied by a contestant merits the score of ippon and indicate the winner by raising his hands towards him after returning both contestants to the places in which they began the contest.

In the case where both contestants score a result which would merit ippon simultaneously (for example strangling techniques) the referee shall announce hiki-wake (draw) and the contestants shall have the right to fight the contest again where necessary.

Commentary

Where a hiki-wake decision has been awarded in accordance with this article and only one contestant wishes to exercise his right to fight the contest again and the other contestant declines the contestant who wishes to fight again should be declared the winner by ippon.

Article 19. Waza-ari (almost ippon)

The referee shall announce waza-ari (almost ippon) when in his opinion the technique applied by a contestant merits the score of waza-ari (almost ippon).

Should one contestant gain a second waza-ari (almost ippon) the referee shall announce instead waza-ari awasete ippon (two waza-aris score ippon) stop the contest and indicate the winner by raising his hands towards him after returning both contestants to the places in which they started the contest.

No Commentary

Article 20. Yuko (almost waza-ari)

The referee shall announce 'yuko' (almost waza-ari) when in his opinion the technique applied by the contestant merits the score of yuko.

Should either contestant score two or further yukos, then the referee shall announce them as they are scored but shall not stop the contest for that reason.

Regardless of how many yukos are announced, no amount will be considered as being equal to a waza-ari. The total number announced will be recorded and used in arriving at the decision whenever a contest is not won by ippon.

Article 21. Koka (almost yuko)

The referee shall announce 'koka' (almost yuko) when in his opinion the technique applied by the contestant merits the score of koka (almost yuko).

Should either contestant score two or further kokas, then the referee shall announce them as they are scored but shall not stop the contest for that reason.

Regardless of how many kokas are announced, no amount will be considered as being equal to a yuko or waza-ari. The total number announced will be recorded and used in arriving at the decision whenever a contest is not won by ippon.

Article 22. Sogo-Gachi (compound win)

The referee shall stop the contest and following the usual procedure indicate the winner after announcing sogo-gachi (compound win) in the following cases:

Where one contestant has gained a waza-ari (almost ippon) and his opponent subsequently receives a penalty of keikoku (warning) or similarly where one contestant whose opponent has already received a penalty of keikoku (warning) is subsequently himself awarded a waza-ari (almost ippon).

No Commentary

Article 23. Osaekomi (holding)

The referee shall announce osaekomi (holding) when in his opinion one contestant is successfully holding the other by a holding technique. The referee shall immediately announce toketa (hold broken) at any time after the announcement of osaekomi (holding) when he considers the hold to be broken.

Commentary

In any case of doubt the referee should ascertain from the time-keepers and then inform the judges of the length of time elapsed between the calls of osaekomi and toketa.

Article 24. Judges unsolicited opinion

Any judge shall indicate by making the appropriate signal whenever he holds a different opinion about an announcement made by the referee. When both judges indicate the same opinion, the judge closest to the referee shall immediately approach him requesting that he stops the contest and rectifies the decision. If the second judge does not hold the same opinion as the first judge, he shall make no signal and the decision of the referee shall prevail.

Commentary

If two judges present an opinion which is different from that of the referee, the referee must announce his decision in accordance with the 'majority of three' rule as in Article 26.

Article 25. Hantei (request for decision)

The referee shall announce sore-made (that is all), stop the contest and return both contestants to their original starting places should the time allotted for the contest expire without there having been a score of ippon.

Should the recorded scores indicate an advantage for either contestant on the following scale—one waza-ari wins over any number of yukos or kokas and when no waza-ari has been scored, one or more yukos wins over any number of kokas (see Article 36(d))—the referee having confirmed which contestant has won, will so indicate by raising his hand towards the winner.

Should the recorded scores either indicate no scores or be exactly the same under each of the headings (waza-ari, yuko, koka), then the referee shall call 'hantei' while raising a hand high in the air. The judges shall in response to this signal, raise either the white or red sign (flag) above their heads in order to indicate which contestant they

Judo

consider merits the decision. To indicate hiki-wake (draw) the judges shall raise the red and white signs (or flags) simultaneously.
No Commentary

Article 26. Declaration of Decision
The referee shall add his own opinion to that indicated by the two judges and shall declare hiki-wake (draw) or yusei-gachi (superiority) according to the majority decision of all three.

Should the opinion of the two judges differ the referee shall make the decision.

When there is only one judge the referee shall take into consideration the opinion of the judge before announcing either yusei-gachi (superiority) or hiki-wake (draw).
Commentary
When the referee has a differing opinion from that of the two judges after having called hantei he may delay giving his decision in order to discuss with them their reasons and thereafter once again shall call hantei and this time must give his decision based upon the majority of three.

Once the referee has announced the result of the contest to the contestants it will not be possible for the referee to change this decision once he has left the competition area.

Should the referee award the victory to the wrong contestant in error the two judges must ensure that he changes this erroneous decision before he leaves the contest area.

Article 27. Application of Matte (wait)
The referee shall announce matte (wait) in order to stop the contest temporarily in the following cases and to recommence the contest shall announce hajime (begin).

Should the referee call jikan (time) or sono-mama (do not move) the time between this announcement and the subsequent recommencement of the contest by the call of either hajime (begin) or yoshi (carry on) shall not count as being part of the time allotted for the contest or the osaekomi (holding).

 (a)   When one or both of the contestants go outside or are about to go outside the contest area.
 (b)   When one or both of the contestants perform or are about to perform one of the prohibited acts.
 (c)   When one or both of the contestants are injured or taken ill.
 (d)   When it is necessary for one or both of the contestants to adjust their costume.
 (e)   When during ne-waza (groundwork) there is no apparent progress and the contestants lie still in a position such as ashi-garami (entangled legs).
 (f)   When in any other case that the referee deems it necessary to do so.
No Commentary

Article 28. Decision After Prohibited Act
Whenever a contest has been decided by hansoku (prohibited act), fusen (default), kiken (withdrawal), injury or accident the referee shall indicate to the contestants the winner of the contest, or if the decision is hiki-wake (draw) the referee shall so

announce the result.
No Commentary

Article 29. Official Signals
The officials shall make gestures as indicated below when taking the following actions:
  (a) **The Referee**
    i   Ippon. Shall raise one of his hands high above his head.
    ii Waza-ari. Shall raise one of his hands, palm down, sideways from his body at shoulder height.
    iii Yuko. Shall raise one of his arms, palm downwards, sideways, 45° from his body.
    iv Koka. Shall raise one of his arms bent with thumb towards the shoulder and elbow at hip level.
    v   Osaekomi. Shall point his arm out away from his body down towards the contestants, while facing the contestants and bending his body towards them.
    vi Osaekomi toketa. Shall raise one of his hands to the front and wave it from right to left quickly two or three times.
    vii To indicate a technique not considered valid, raise one of his hands above his head to the front and wave it from right to left two or three times.
    viii Hiki-wake. Raise one of his hands high in the air and bring it down to the front of his body (with thumb edge up) and hold it there for a while.
    ix Jikan. Raise one of his hands to shoulder height and with the arm approximately parallel to the tatami display the flattened palm of his hand with the fingers up to the time keeper.
    x   To indicate that in his opinion either or both of the contestants are guilty of 'non-combativity' the referee shall raise both his hands to chest height in front of his body and rotate both hands around each other in the direction of the offending contestant or contestants.
  (b) **The Judges**
    i   To indicate that he considers a contestant has stayed within the contest area the judge shall raise one of his hands up in the air and bring it down to shoulder height along the boundary line of the contest area generally with the thumb upwards and momentarily hold it there.
    ii To indicate that in his opinion one of the contestants is out of the contest area the judge shall raise one of his hands to shoulder height along the boundary line of the contest area generally with the thumb edge upwards and wave it from right to left several times.

Commentary
The above signals should generally be held for a minimum of three seconds.

Article 30. Prohibited Acts
All the following acts are forbidden.

(a) To sweep the opponent's supporting leg from the inside when the opponent is applying a technique such as harai-goshi (sweeping loin).

(b) To attempt to throw the opponent with kawazu-gake (throwing the opponent with one leg entwined around his).

(c) To apply the action of dojime (leg scissors) to the opponent's trunk, neck or head.

(d) To apply kansetsu-waza (joint locks) anywhere other than the elbow joint.

(e) To apply any action which might injure the neck or spinal vertebrae of the opponent.

(f) To lift off the mat an opponent who is lying on his back in order to drive him back into the mat.

(g) To intentionally fall backwards when the other contestant is clinging to your back and when either contestant has control of the other's movement.

(h) To kick with the knee or foot the hand or arm of the opponent in order to make him release his grasp.

(i) To intentionally avoid taking hold of the opponent in order to prevent action in the contest.

(j) To intentionally go outside of or force the opponent to go outside of the contest area.

(k) To go outside the contest area from the standing position for ANY REASON except as a result of a technique or action of the opponent.

(l) To adopt an excessively defensive attitude.

(m) To hold continually the opponent's collar, lapel or sleeve on the same side with both hands or the opponent's belt or the bottom of his jacket with either or both hands.

(n) To insert a finger or fingers inside the opponent's sleeve or the bottom of his trousers or to grasp by 'screwing up' his sleeve.

(o) To stand continually with the fingers of one or both hands interlocked in order to prevent action in the contest.

(p) To intentionally disarrange his own judogi (judo costume) or to untie or retie the belt of the trousers without the referee's permission.

(q) To pull the opponent down in order to start ne-waza (groundwork).

(r) To take hold of the opponent's leg or foot in order to change to ne-waza (groundwork) unless exceptional skill is shown.

(s) To wind the end of the belt or jacket around any part of the opponent's body.

(t) To take the opponent's judogi (judo costume) in the mouth or to put a hand or arm or foot or leg directly on the opponent's face.

(u) To put a foot or leg in the opponent's belt, collar or lapel or to bend back the opponent's finger or fingers in order to break the opponent's grip.

(v) To maintain (not let go) whilst lying on the back a hold with the legs round the neck and armpit of the opponent when the opponent succeeds in standing or gets to his knees in a position from which he could lift up the contestant.

(w) To attempt to apply any technique outside the contest area.

(x) To disregard the referee's instructions.

(y) To make unnecessary calls, remarks or gestures derogatory to the opponent during the contest.

(z) To make any other action which may injure or endanger the opponent or may be against the spirit of judo.

Any contestant who performs or attempts to perform any of the above acts shall be liable for disqualification or other disciplinary action by the referee in accordance with theses rules.

Commentary

Notwithstanding Article 4 (Location) if the referee has the opinion that a contestant has intentionally and against the spirit of judo thrown his opponent out of the contest area he should be penalised.

In relation to paragraph (I) of this article, a state of non-combativity may be taken to exist when in general for 20 to 30 seconds there have been no attacking moves on the part of one of either or both contestants. This period may be prolonged or shortened depending upon the circumstances.

Article 31. Penalties

The referee shall declare shido (note), chui (caution), keikoku (warning) or hansoku-make (disqualification) according to the gravity of any infringement of the regulations in Article 30. In general a simple repetition of an infringement in one of the above mentioned categories shall merit a penalty of the next highest category.

If chui (caution) is announced to one contestant the other shall be regarded as having scored yuko (almost waza-ari). Similarly if keikoku (warning) is awarded to one contestant the other shall be considered as having been awarded waza-ari (almost ippon).

Should the referee award chui (caution) he shall temporarily stop the contest, return the contestants to the standing position in which they started the contest, and announce chui (caution) whilst raising his hands towards the contestant who committed the prohibited act.

Should the referee award keikoku (warning) he shall temporarily stop the contest, return the contestants to the standing position in which they started the contest and after making them adopt the correct sitting position shall announce keikoku (warning) whilst raising his hand towards the contestant who committed the prohibited act.

However if the referee has called osaekomi and it is the contestant being held down who commits the offence meriting a keikoku, then the referee shall call sono-mama, announce the keikoku in the osaekomi position and then recommence the contest by calling yoshi.

Commentary

(1) Shido is generally given to any contestant who is about to infringe or who has already committed a very slight infringement of Article 30 (Prohibited Acts). Chui is generally given to any contestant who repeats a very slight infringement or commits a moderate infringement of Article 30.

Keikoku is generally given to any contestant who repeats a moderate infringement or commits a serious infringement of Article 30.

Hansoku-make is generally given to any contestant who repeats a serious infringement or who commits a very grave infringement of Article 30.

(2) Where both contestants infringe the rules at the same time each should be awarded a penalty according to the degree of the infringement.

(3) Where both contestants have already been awarded keikoku and subsequently each receive a further penalty they should both be declared hansoku-make. Nonetheless the officials may make their final decision in this matter in accordance with Article 41 (Situations not covered by these rules).

(4) Where a contestant infringes paragraph 'j' or 'k' of Article 30 the penalty awarded should be as follows:

(a) Where one contestant deliberately leaves the contest area or pretends to apply a technique in order to leave the contest area the penalty given should be keikoku.

(b) Where a contestant deliberately forces his opponent out of the contest area (including the case referred to in the commentary to Article 30) the penalty should be keikoku.

(c) If a contestant leaves the contest area due to his own efforts to upset his opponent's balance the penalty awarded should be chui. However if he leaves the contest area as the result of an action by his opponent he should not be penalised.

(5) The first warning by the referee (Article 29(a)x) that he considers that either or both of the contestants are guilty of non-combativity should not entail the awarding of any penalty to the contestants so warned. Subsequent warnings (Article 30(x)) should entail awarding penalties in accordance with the article to which this commentary applies.

(6) (a) Where one contestant pulls his opponent down into ne-waza not in accordance with Article 9 and his opponent does not take advantage of this to continue into ne-waza, the referee shall call matte, stop the contest and award chui to the contestant who has infringed Article 9.

(b) Where one contestant pulls his opponent down into ne-waza not in accordance with the rules of Article 9 and his opponent takes advantage of this to continue into ne-waza, the contest should be allowed to continue but the referee should award chui to the contestant who has infringed Article 9.

(7) Before awarding keikoku or hansoku-make the referee must consult with the judges and make his decision in accordance with the majority of three.

(8) Penalties are not cumulative. Each penalty must be awarded at its own value. The awarding of any second or subsequent penalty automatically cancels any earlier penalty. Whenever a contestant has already been penalised, any succeeding penalties for that contestant must always be awarded at least in the next higher value than his existing penalty.

Article 32. Assessment of Ippon

The decision of ippon (full point) shall be given in the following cases:

(a) **Nage-waza (throwing techniques)**

  i When the contestant applying a technique or countering his opponent's attacking technique throws his opponent largely on his back with considerable force or impetus.

  ii When a contestant skilfully lifts his opponent who is lying with his back on the mat up to about the height of his own shoulders.

(b) **Katame-waza (grappling techniques)**

  i When one contestant says maitta (I give up) or taps his or his opponent's body or the mat with his hand or foot twice or more.

  ii When one contestant holds the other, who is unable to get away, for 30 seconds, after the announcement of osaekomi (holding).

  iii Where the effect of a technique of shime-waza (strangle) or kansetsu-waza (lock) is sufficiently apparent.

Commentary

Where one contestant who is holding his opponent by an osaekomi-waza which has been 'called' changes without loss of control into another or succeeding osaekomi-waza the time shall be allowed to continue until ippon has been declared or the opponent succeeds in escaping.

Article 33. Assessment of Waza-ari

The decision of waza-ari (almost ippon) shall be given in the following cases:

(a) **Nage-waza (throwing techniques)**

  When a contestant applying a throwing technique is not completely successful (for example, the technique is lacking in any one of the three elements of: largely on his back, force or impetus) and does not quite merit the score of ippon.

(b) **Osaekomi-waza (grappling techniques)**

  When one contestant is holding another as in Article 32 (b) ii for 25 seconds or more but less than 30 seconds.

Commentary

Where one contestant tries tomoe-nage but is temporarily unsuccessful and then after an appreciable time whilst still on his back subsequently succeeds in completing tomoe-nage he shall only be able to score a maximum of waza-ari because the throw is now being done from a lying and not a standing position.

Article 34. Assessment of Yuko

The decision of yuko (almost waza-ari) shall be given in the following cases:

(a) **Nage-waza (throwing techniques)**

  When a contestant applying a throwing technique is only partially successful, for example is lacking more than is required to score waza-ari, of one of the three elements of: largely on the back, force or impetus, and does not quite

merit the score of waza-ari.
  (b) **Osaekomi-waza (grappling techniques)**
  When one contestant is holding another, as in Article 32 (b) ii, for 20 seconds or more, but less than 25 seconds.

Article 35.   Assessment of Koka
The decision of koka (almost yuko) shall be given in the following cases:
  (a) **Nage-waza (throwing techniques)**
  When a contestant makes a throwing technique which is not successful, but with some force or impetus puts his opponent on to his side, thigh(s), stomach or buttocks and does not quite merit the score of yuko.
  (b) **Osaekomi-waza (grappling techniques)**
  When one contestant is holding another for 10 seconds or more but less than 20 seconds.
Commentary
Throwing an opponent on to his knee(s), hand(s) or elbow(s) will only be counted as the same as any other attack. Similarly an osaekomi of up to nine seconds will be counted as an attack.

Article 36.   Assessment of Yusei-gachi
The decision if yusei-gachi (superiority win) shall generally be given in the following cases:
  (a) Where there has been a score of waza-ari (almost ippon) or a penalty of keikoku (warning).
  (b) Where there has been a score of yuko (almost waza-ari) or chui (caution).
  (c) Where there has been a score of koka (almost yuko) or shido (note).
  (d) Where all scores as recorded in Article 25 are equal for both contestants, the yusei-gachi shall be given to the contestant who has the least severe penalty recorded against him.
  (e) Where there is a recognisable difference in the attitude during the contest or in the skill and effectiveness of technique.
Commentary
  (a) The criteria for deciding where yusei-gachi wins should be dispensed with entirely or should be applied according to either (a), (b), (c) or (d) above is the responsibility of the organising committee for each particular event and officials should ascertain before taking their places on the mat under which conditions yusei-gachi is to be given.

Article 37.   Assessment of Hiki-wake
The decision of hiki-wake (draw) shall be given when there is no positive score and where it is impossible to judge the superiority of either contestant in accordance with Article 36 above within the time allotted for the contest.
No Commentary

Article 38.   Assessment of Hansoku-make
The decision of hansoku-make (disqualification) should be given:
  (a) Where one contestant has had the penalty of keikoku (warning) awarded against him and then receives a further penalty.
  (b) Where any act on the part of one contestant gravely infringes Article 30 above (Prohibited Acts) as for example where any act on his part may injure or endanger his opponent or any remark or gesture, etc., of his is considered to be contrary to the principles of judo.
No Commentary

Article 39.   Default and Withdrawal
The decision of fusen-gachi (win by default) shall be given to any contestant whose opponent does not appear for his contest.
   The decision of kiken-gachi (win by withdrawal) shall be given to any contestant whose opponent withdraws from the competition during the contest.
No Commentary

Article 40.   Injury, Illness or Accident
In every case where a competition is stopped because of injury to either or both of the contestants, the referee and judges may permit a maximum time of five minutes to the injured player(s) for recuperation.
   The decision of kachi (win), make (loss), hiki-wake (draw) where one contestant is unable to continue because of injury, illness or accident during the contest shall be given by the referee after consultation with the judges according to the following clauses:
  (a) **Injury**
          Where the cause of the injury is attributed to the injured contestant he shall lose the contest.
      ii   Where the cause of the injury is attributed to the uninjured contestant the uninjured contestant shall lose the contest.
      iii Where it is impossible to attribute the cause of injury to either contestant the decision of hiki-wake (draw) may be given.
  (b) **Sickness**
        Generally where one contestant is taken sick during a contest and is unable to continue he shall lose the contest.
  (c) **Accident**
        Where an accident occurs which is due to an outside influence the decision hiki-wake (draw) shall be given.
Commentary
Should a doctor advise a contestant to withdraw from a competition and the contestant does not wish to do so the referee should ensure that the contestant first signs a release or waiver of responsibility.

63

Judo

Article 41.   Situations Not Covered by the Rules
Where any situation arises which is not covered by these rules it shall be dealt with and a decision given by the referee after consultation with the judges.
No Commentary

Reprinted by courtesy of the International Judo Federation